The Wheels on the Bus

To Alice Kovalski

Kids Can Press Ltd. gratefully
acknowledges the assistance of the
Canada Council and the Ontario Arts
Council in the production of this book.

Canadian Cataloguing in Publication Data
Kovalski, Maryann.
  The wheels on the bus

ISBN 0-921103-09-3 (bound) ISBN 0-921103-92-1 (pbk.)

I. Title.

PS8571.096W48 1987   jC813'.54   C87-093497-X
PZ7.K87Wh 1987

Text and Illustrations Copyright © 1987 by
Maryann Kovalski
Musical notation by Miriam Katzin

Kids Can Press Ltd.,
585½ Bloor Street West,
Toronto, Ontario, Canada, M6G 1K5.

Printed by Everbest Printing Co., Ltd.,
Hong Kong

PA 89 0 9 8 7 6 5

Maryann Kovalski

The Wheels on the Bus

Kids Can Press Ltd.
Toronto

One day, Grandma took Jenny and Joanna shopping for new winter coats.

They tried on long coats and short coats, blue coats and red coats, plaid coats and even rain coats. Joanna chose a coat with wooden barrel buttons. Jenny liked it too, because of the hood.

When it was time to go home, the bus didn't come for a long time and everyone grew tired. "I have an idea, sweeties," said Grandma. "Let's sing a song my Granny sang with me when I was a little girl." And so they began to sing . . .

The wheels on the bus go round and

round round and round round and

round. The wheels on the bus go

round and round all

around the town.

The wipers on the bus go swish, swish, swish
   swish, swish, swish
   swish, swish, swish
The wipers on the bus go swish, swish, swish
   all around the town.

The people on the bus hop on and off
   on and off
   on and off
The people on the bus hop on and off
   all around the town.

The horn on the bus goes toot, toot, toot
   toot, toot, toot
   toot, toot, toot
The horn on the bus goes toot, toot, toot
   all around the town.

The money on the bus goes clink, clink, clink
    clink, clink, clink
    clink, clink, clink
The money on the bus goes clink, clink, clink
    all around the town.

The people on the bus go up and down
    up and down
    up and down
The people on the bus go up and down
    all around the town.

The babies on the bus go waaa, waaa, waaa
   waaa, waaa, waaa
   waaa, waaa, waaa
The babies on the bus go waaa, waaa, waaa
   all around the town.

The parents on the bus go ssh, ssh, ssh
    ssh, ssh, ssh
    ssh, ssh, ssh
The parents on the bus go ssh, ssh, ssh
    all around the town.

The wheels on the bus go round and round
  round and round
  round and round
The wheels on the bus go round and round
  all around the town.

Grandma, Jenny and Joanna had so much fun singing
that . . .

They missed the bus!   So . . .

They took a taxi.

The end